Other Books by Eric Krimmel

Jimland

The Cross Country Adventures of the
Blue Highways Cycling Elite

Illuminate: The yearlong photo-a-day project

Uncut Garden

www.erickrimmel.com

Copyright

Fiction
This a work of fiction. Any resemblence to persons, places, or
locales, is entirely coincidental.

First edition- Print version

www.erickrimmel.com

15 Moments

Eric Krimmel

Acknowledgements

I wish to express my thanks to Ann Cook, and Anita O'Brien for their assistance in editing this work.

www.erickrimmel.com

Contents

I hear you do these kind of things

It almost always starts the same way: the phone rings and the person on the other end says, "I've got a situation..." Which might be okay if it was the President and he wanted me to parachute into a third world country, disarm a nuclear bomb and was willing to pay a seven-figure fee. But it isn't.

And it almost always ends with, "I hear you do these kind of things."

The last situation, "I'm pretty sure one of my waitresses flushed her cell phone down our only toilet." No, you don't ask how this stuff happens and I don't want to know how he knows.

"I've snaked it and plunged it and it's not overflowing but I can't ask my customers to pee only, if you get what I mean." All too well. In a small diner with one restroom that has only one toilet, this is a catastrophe.

I show up, don my rubber gloves, unbolt the toilet, pull it up and set it aside. I glance down the hole in the floor. The water is not at floor level but down a ways so the phone is probably not stuck there. I grab the toilet, dump the excess water, and set it on its side. I reach up underneath through some goo and find the phone wedged in there and almost have to break it to get it out– not that it's ever going to work again or that anyone would want to use it if it did.

I scrape off the old wax ring, lay down a new one, position the toilet and bolt it down. In a few minutes I leave with enough money to make it worth my while but about a fraction of what a professional plumber would charge, which is why I get calls like this. Not enough to make a living but often enough to make life interesting. Not in the fun kind of way, but in the way that makes me think, Perhaps this is what was meant when it was said that to be a good writer you should live an interesting life.

Jane

As I've gotten older I've found that I can't remember things like I used to. At first I thought it was age and the way the brain is supposed to lose some of it's effectiveness over time. But then I realized there are new things to remember every single day. Things are added to my memory at an astonishing rate, without being aware of it.

So as I'm learning new things everyday, I realize that my memory just can't hold all the information. It's like a hard drive that fills up and can't accept any more data unless some is erased. Or like a large tank that holds drops of information. When the tank is full the excess just spills over. It's random. You don't get a chance to decide what is kept and what is ejected. I remember the name of the owner of Mister Ed, the talking horse, from that TV series. It's Wilbur. How useless is that? Even if I could justify the retention by saying I might need it to win some trivia contest I would gladly concede to have that block of memory back. Please, will you just spill over the edge so I can retain something worthwhile?

Also, it's easy to forget that we are storing information that we take for granted. Information that we need and use regularly. Things that are key to our survival like, corn is good to eat but poison ivy isn't. Or that a red light means that you have to press that one pedal, which one, oh yes now I remember, the one on the left to bring the car to a stop. And you have remember to do it in a timely manner, and it's good to remember the consequences of forgetting something like that. So these kind of things are taking up space too, and I'm glad I haven't forgotten them.

But when it comes to Jane, I'm annoyed that I have to take up precious space by remembering that if she chews gum in the car she'll throw up, because for some reason she's always chewing it and she never remembers. Then all of a sudden, boop! there's a little vomit on the seat or the carpet or her clothes and that's just not a pleasant thing. Or the fact that breast cancer runs in her family and she needs to be examined regularly. Maybe she remembers and just doesn't want to go. Or maybe she's just pushing it out of her memory because the thought of it is just too frightful.

I remember all of the commands of that silly computer game that I never play because she's always asking me how to operate it.

And she just can't remember any phone number no matter how many times she dials it. It certainly doesn't help our relationship when she asks and I say "Just look it up," when she knows that I know it. One of these days we'll get a phone that stores all our important numbers to replace the vintage one we keep on the stand next to her favorite chair in the living room. I only wish I had enough memory available to hold that thought when I go to the store.

Then there's all the small stuff like when her birthday is or when our anniversary is or the kind of flowers she likes or all the names of her friends and relatives and all their quirky habits and interests. It's kind of important to remember that stuff even though it's clogging up a good portion of my brain.

If I just didn't have to hold on to this stuff I could retain all kinds of important information and wouldn't forget things like the name of the person I just met two minutes ago. Or I could use it for complex scientific theories and abstracts of philosophical concepts, things that would make me appear smarter than I am. Then I could really impress people with relevant facts and pertinent knowledge, so much the better if they didn't understand what I was saying.

But then I see her sitting patiently at a table in a restaurant where we are supposed to meet for lunch and the radiant smile that welcomes me. Or I feel her warm naked body lying on top of me and the faint smell of that floral perfume mixed with her natural scent. Or she'll say something nonchalantly, that is, in fact, an amazing insight from a perspective I just couldn't imagine. Or she'll look at me in a way that is simply captivating, or say something so hilarious that I can barely catch my breath I'm laughing so hard.

And then I think that it's not such a bad thing, giving up some of my precious memory for her. In fact it's a rather small price to pay at all.

Merry Christmas!

"So you're just supposed to run it up and down your leg?"

"Yeah, I guess, just like in the commercial."

It was Christmas morning and my sisters were anxious to try their new gift before we had to get ready for our guests. Two of them were old enough to shave their legs and a third would soon be.

Ann turned the device on and touched her leg. "OW!" She quickly jerked it away.

"What's wrong?" Melissa asked.

"It *hurts!*"

"Maybe you're just doing it wrong. You have to rub it back and forth."

"It hurts when I touch the skin!"

"Don't just set it on you leg."

"I'm not!"

"Try again. And keep it moving."

Ann slowly moved the device toward her leg, stopped, then in a downward, brushing motion lightly lowered it to the skin.

"AH!" She blurted out as she cringed and pulled her leg back. She turned it off and thrust it toward Melissa. "Here, you try it!"

Melissa looked at the coiled metal on the end, the part that removes the hair. "Maybe we just don't have it set properly." Neither one wanted to let go of the fantasy, promising quick, easy, and painless hair removal. Since it hadn't worked according to their desire, now was the time to look at the instructions. Melissa dug them out of the box and started reading.

A silent moment later, she shrugged and handed them to Ann. The instructions were brief and little more than what could be figured out with common sense.

"Well," Melissa said, "we must be doing something wrong." She picked up the box searching for further clues. "How could they sell something like this if it didn't work?"

"Oh, it works," I said, smiling. "The fact that it would probably be better used as an implement of torture, doesn't mean that the claims of hair removal are false. Think about it, it's ripping the hair out at the root. How could something like that not hurt?"

"But in the commercial they are just running it up and down their leg," Ann said.

"Yeah, but it wouldn't be the first time a commercial was misleading." I was trying to think of how the company might have shot it without the actors shrieking in pain. "Maybe they didn't turn it on, or maybe they had already shaved their legs. I don't know."

"Try it on your leg," Melissa said to me with a smile on her face.

"With all the hair I have? No way!"

"C'mon," Melissa said chucking. "It won't hurt."

"Never!" We were laughing.

"Maybe it just hurts at first, then you get used to it," Melissa said in a serious tone. Being the older sister, she liked to get Ann to try things she was afraid of. I didn't know if she was really looking for a solution or just egging Ann on. "Here Ann, I'll turn it down to the lowest setting."

"I'm not doing it again!"

"Oh, go on. It's on the lowest setting and remember to keep it moving."

With a little prodding Ann decided to give it another try. She turned it on and slowly moved it closer to her skin. Her whole body tensed up. She held it there for a few seconds then jerked it forward and covered a good 8 inches of her shin. "AAAAH!"

"Did it feel any better?"

"No! It was worse!"

Everyone but Ann was laughing. "It's not funny," she said while rubbing her leg.

"No," I said, trying to gather my composure, "it's not. But it's like, 'Here, hit yourself on the head with this hammer. Did it hurt? Well, try hitting yourself 5 times with the hammer because that might not hurt as much.'" We all burst out laughing.

Mom was in the dining room and overheard our conversation. She walked over and sat down in the rocking chair near us as if she was fed up with our foolishness and was going to show everyone how it's done.

"Let's see them," she bluntly said, sticking out her hand and referring to the instructions. A few seconds later, "Give it to me." She ran her thumb along the part that contacted the skin and convinced that it was harmless, pulled up her ankle-length skirt, turned it on, and in a sweeping motion brushed it down her leg. A high pitched scream followed, as she pulled it away and yanked her leg back. "What's wrong with this?"

My sisters and I howled with delight.

Ann, trying to be the diplomat, said, "Mom, the box says, 'You may experience mild discomfort.'" We laughed hard again.

"Mild discomfort? Bull-SHIT!" She declared definitively, flicked it off and tossed it on the carpet.

When we caught our breath, Melissa, still not wanting to give up on the idea of easy, painless hair removal said, "Maybe someone at school has one and I can ask them about it." She gathered everything and put it back in the box.

Eventually she did ask around but her friend's stories weren't any different than ours. The device was stored away, though occasionally reminded my sisters that, yes, it was as painful as they remembered.

It's not that I cared

It's not that I cared, but I really did.

Julie spotted me in the bookstore and walked up while I was deep in a travel guide on the Himalayas. It was good to see her. It had been long enough to notice that she was wearing a dress, carrying a purse and sporting a hair style I had never seen.

Both of us were smiling profusely. We made small talk about friends and family without going into too much detail of the day-to-day changes and drama. I told her I had moved and she told me about her promotion at work. Then, not wanting our brief encounter to end, I asked if she was taking a lot of pictures.

When we were together, she would remorsefully talk about not having photos of past events or not enough of the important moments in her life. Just before the end, I picked out a camera that was easy to use and had the features she wanted. I thought it was a pertinent gift.

"No," she said, "but John is," and laughed.

He was the new boyfriend.

"He uses it for work," she added. I remembered he was a realtor because he wasn't only the new boyfriend, he was the old one too, the one before me.

"But that's about it. We just never seem to remember when things come up," she said expressing herself in an 'Oh well,' kind of way.

"But he really likes it," then trying to sound more upbeat.

The camera was something that I thought would bring her joy

time and again by having a record of those important events in her life, but it was only now that I realized I had missed the mark. What she really wanted was for someone to take the photos for her, which of course I did, when we were together. I couldn't tell if Julie was being thoughtless, or purposely hurtful, or really just thought the situation was funny.

There was a pause as I remembered other things about Julie and it now surprised me to think that she was the one who wanted to move on when I didn't.

"Hey, did that pillow help your stiff neck?" she said.

Julie had tried quite a few pillows before she had come across what she considered was the ultimate, and when she gave me one, was so excited it sounded like it was the panacea for a good night's sleep. But it was too soft for me and I could never get used to it.

I could have just said yes. I could have lied and said something very complimentary. Instead, I told the truth.

"No. But Clair is getting a lot of use out of it," and smiled half heartedly.

It was only then that she realized the impact of her flippancy in regards to the remarks she made about the camera and all of a sudden it wasn't so funny after all.

It's not that such things really matter, but they do.

G8

It was 2002 and NASA was having a hissy fit over Russia selling rides to, and a stay on, the International Space Station, in order to help pay for their portion of it. George W. Bush was settling in to his first term in office and building an alliance with Tony Blair, the Prime Minister of the United Kingdom, as they were preparing for the G8 Summit, a conference of the leaders of the 8 largest industrial nations.

Around this time I had the good fortune to be invited to one of those exclusive, high class parties. It was in a stately old mansion, the kind with ornate craftsmanship that the rich wouldn't spend money on today, even if they could find the artisans to build it. It wasn't a museum like so many are these days, the hosts actually lived there.

The event was stunning, the attention to detail and the level of extravagance was something you didn't think still existed, and the guests were accommodating. The main room was filled with high society women, some in dresses that cost more than a car. In general, the crowd was prim and highly educated but the kind of people who were more concerned with the model of jet you owned and the length of your yacht, than the integrity of your character.

I noticed one woman making the rounds, not the hostess, I had met her shortly after I had arrived, but my guess, the Queen of Gossip. There were only a few at the party she was not familiar with and I was one of them. I mingled and made party chitchat with a few of the guests until she approached me and without introducing herself said, "And who are you?"

I gave her my name and extended my hand.

She looked somewhat confused, "How nice for you," and lightly pinched my fingertips between her thumb and fingertips as if this were an acceptable form of handshake. What she was really asking for was my title and celebrity status.

It would have been a faux pas to ask me what my occupation was since I was probably the only person at the party who had to work for a living. As she sized me up, obviously sensing my rented apparel, she turned away and without looking at me said, "So, what do you do for fun?"

I couldn't resist. What I lacked in net worth I could make up in wit. "Well, the climbing season on Mt Everest this year was so short it left hundreds stranded but we made it to the summit, of course, and the view is really indescribable." I took a sip of champagne and continued.

"My trip to the northern reaches of the Amazon Rainforest resulted in nearly 40 discoveries of previously unknown plants and insects. The cure to alzheimer's, cancer, ebola, could be locked inside any one of them." I was mimicking her body language standing side by side, looking out toward the crowd and fully aware she could hear everything I was saying.

"Oh! The space station was a fantastic experience! And let me tell you, those cosmonauts are such partiers! What a great group of guys. One of them even introduced me to Putin. He wants me to come to the G8 summit. Man, is that guy a party boy! You get a few bottles of vodka in him and he'll tell you all kinds of Russian secrets. As a matter of fact, don't tell anyone this…" I paused briefly and turned my head toward her. She couldn't resist making eye contact, then I turned away, looking back out toward the crowd. "Well, that's classified and with the NSA monitoring my every move these days I have to be careful about what I say. I'll tell you in private."

"Anyway, the G8. I don't think I'm going to go. I mean it's just so trying listening to Bush and Blair blah, blah, blahing about AIDS in Africa, gross domestic product, international trade, and canceling third world debt as if they actually ran the countries they were elected to serve. It would drive anyone to drink, not that Putin needs an excuse. He'll get so drunk eventually he's going to barf and it'll come when you least expect it so you don't want to be wearing a good pair of shoes around him or they'll be ruined. I mean, after hours the whole thing turns into one big party, so what do you expect? Now when Blair gets drunk he loses the accent, turns out it's fake. Who knew? He just used it to win votes and now he's stuck with it.

And I guarantee Schroder will be whining again about the cost of reuniting the Fatherland, and what a drain the east side has been. It's just so tedious. Suck it up, buttercup! If you didn't want it, you should have let Russia keep it.

Then there's Chirac. He's always so pompous and self righteous but awhile back we were hanging out one night and you know what he was drinking? Gallo! Turns out he loves the stuff and has it shipped in by the ton.

Now let me give you some advice. If you ever meet him, stand back. The whole bloody country is radioactive because of all the nuclear power they use. If you shake his hand, 10 years down the road you'll get hand cancer, I'm sure of it.

Those high profile events really aren't what they're cracked up to be. So yeah, I think I'll pass. But the space station, you should check it out."

Echoes from a presence now gone

I see her lying there beside the easy chair, her two white paws extending out from just the other side. When I come home she's frantically wagging her tail and whimpering full of excitement and anticipation as I sort through my keys and insert the right one. She doesn't like the sound of the lawn mower and when I get close, she emerges from the low branches of the blue spruce where she likes to lay when it's hot.

In each case I momentarily pause– incoherent, body limp, as my brain recalibrates.

She's gone.

The two white paws in the dimly lit basement are a pair of white tennis shoes. It's a piece of paper that the wind blows out from under the tree where she used to lie that mimics her white chest in contrast to her black coat when I last cut the grass. It's not a hallucination but the established routine that invades my mind, as I walk up to the door while thinking about work or other things, so quickly that I have no time to conscientiously form a thought before feeling the excitement she does. Hearing the sharp snap of the lock I realize she's not there, and never will be.

Size 8

When it comes to sizes, women are foolish. It's not their fault, our culture makes them crazy over this issue, but that doesn't make it easier on the rest of us.

I used to work in the shoe department at a sporting goods store and women would come in and say something like, "I want to see this in a size 6." I'd go in the back and bring out the pair, then they would try to cram their foot into a shoe that is obviously too small. So then the woman would say, "Oh these must run small." No! It's that you're trying to fit those boats into a shoe that's way too tiny, big foot! But I couldn't say that, so I didn't.

The thing is, shoes can't run small. Shoes are sized according to a universal last, a shoe mold for each size that all companies use. It's like an inch or a quart, a predetermined measurement. A milk company can't put less milk in a jug and claim it's a gallon, a gallon is a specific quantity. With shoes, there can be a slight variation based on manufacturing techniques or materials, but a size 7 is going to be a size 7 from any company.

Now clothing is different. Sizes like medium and large at one time corresponded to a specific body size, but no longer. And dress sizes were universal too, but then Relaxed Fit and Oversized created different proportions and apparel companies realized they could sell more clothes if they made them bigger without changing the labels. It's all marketing. It makes women feel better and more likely to buy if they think they can fit into a smaller size. Except it's not smaller it just has a tag claiming it's smaller. And some companies take this to the extreme.

So knowing all this can cause problems...

My girlfriend comes home and she excitedly shows me the dress she just bought. It's hideous. I'm not a fashion expert but I still know enough to know this dress is hideous. But I can't exactly say that.

"It's nice," *Be careful* "but," *Be careful* "it's not exactly your style." *Hey, not too bad.*

"But it's a 4!" She says excitedly. "I fit into a 4!"

I look at her with that, Really? Are you really that dumb? look on my face. Good thing I didn't say that.

"What?" she says. And it's a good thing she can't read my mind. *But it doesn't matter because you're dumb enough to tell her.*

"It's not a 4." *Oh, goody. If we are going to play with a bomb let's make it a nuclear one.*

"Yes it is. Look." She grabs the tag at the back of the dress. It clearly says 4. *Let it go, let it go, let it go...*

"Yeah. But it's not a 4." *Oooh!* I know this because she is a very attractive 8. And I know she is an 8 because we've been shopping together and I've bought her things and I got the right size because she, herself, told me her size. *It doesn't matter if you're technically right...*

She looks at me as if she doesn't understand why I'm saying the dress is not a 4. I can't contain my frustration any longer and in the most sympathetic voice I can muster, *Your intonation isn't going to matter either...* say, "Sweetheart, you're not a 4. You weren't a 4 when you tried on that dress. You weren't a 4 when you walked into that store. You weren't a 4 when you woke up this morning. You weren't a 4 last week or last month or last year or when we first started dating." *Oops, went too far. Yeah, way too far.*

She looks at me with a scowl on her face and fire in her eyes. *The Titanic is sinking! Quick!*

Pleading, I say, "This is clearly a marketing scam! Companies keep making clothing bigger without upgrading the size. A 4 today is bigger than it used to be and you can't compare a 4 from one company to another any more." *You're going to try to use logic to disrupt her fantasy? Good luck!*

In a deep, low voice she says, "Oh. You just think I'm fat." *Ooooooooooo* "And dumb." *Well, if the shoe fits… NO, DON'T YOU DARE!*

After a comment like that there is no good place this conversation is going, so it's better to bite your tongue. *Finally!* Staring at her with my mouth half open for a few seconds, I quickly say, "I have to go cut the grass," and with that I run out of the house.

This kind of situation is going to come up again, so for future reference, what you need to say is something like, "Looks great! Good job!"

Of course, that's not what I said.

Maybe next time.

Stalked by death

There are those who say they can speak to the dead. Beyond the obvious charlatans, there seem to be ones who have an ability that science can't explain. If it's a trick, it's a pretty elaborate one. They are good enough to tell you things they could never know. Among the ones that are first rate and have yet to be discredited, is the common belief that about 6 months before you are going to die you receive messages that warn you. Whether they come from God or some form of god or the universe, is immaterial. You can ignore them like most people do or you can use the time to prepare yourself to pass into another existence. It's said that you can hear these messages if you listen for them. But is it possible to separate divine intervention from everyday coincidence?

Carl looked up at the clock at the pizzeria and said, "If things don't pick up by 9:00, I'm gonna call it."

He had never used that expression before and Bob knew he wasn't talking about closing. He looked at Carl with a sense of unease. "What do you mean?"

Carl shrugged and said, "There'll be no use keeping you on if we're not busy. You're done. You're outta here."

Were they just expressions or was the universe trying to tell Bob something? He was just wondering, because a while back he started noticing how many people said "Good bye" and not "See ya," or "Talk to you later." It was a lot more than in the past.

It would be easy to brush this stuff off, he thought, but just last week all of his deliveries added up to $666.00. They have to add up to something and this is not an unusually a large or small amount, but just this number, in this context, was unsettling.

Then there's that guy he'd been delivering pizzas to who lives at 666 Cherry Street, a dead end street, as someone pointed out. The crew at the pizzeria jokingly referred to him as the devil, but now it didn't seem so funny. He is old and grisly, his face always sporting a four day growth, never less, never more. He couldn't survive without the transparent tube hooked to his nose that carries oxygen from the tank he rolls behind him. In spite of his condition the house has a smell of stale cigarettes that is overwhelming. How could he smoke in that condition, unless... Just makes you wonder.

Not surprisingly, the devil is gruff but not an unpleasant man since it would be hard to lure people to the dark side if you were. And, well, you didn't really think he would show up with horns and a pitchfork, did you?

There are no deals to be made, he is more interested in satisfying his hunger than the state of Bob's soul. But was this another sign that the end was near?

This all might seem rather silly but for some reason, about two months ago, Bob started thinking about writing a will. It's not that he has much to divide up. He was thinking who would get the car, who would get the computer, things like that. Then he started to feel uneasy. If his friends and family searched through his laptop would they think less of him? If he didn't get a chance to erase the history on his browser they would see that he had recently visited a porn site. If they went through his writing would they understand the dark and obscure and wild stuff? And what about all those great ideas that he hadn't developed yet. Would one of his friends, or rather his so-called friends, steal his ideas and eventually win the god damn Nobel Prize with an idea he didn't get a chance to develop?

Reflecting on his life he began to feel melancholy. Much to his chagrin, Bob felt his obit would be easy to write: "Pretty much wasted his life. Nothing of any merit to mention." This had been a perpetual monkey on his back; dreams unachieved, ideas undeveloped. But was the fact that he was even thinking about this stuff a message from the universe that the end was near?

Bob thought this might make a good story, that he could include it in his short story collection. Then panic gripped him- was the very idea of writing about this one more sign?

As Bob laid in bed, clearly wound up with the very thought that his life could soon be over, it was well past midnight as he tossed and turned in a state of panic, afraid to close his eyes, convinced that if he did it would be for the last time. He hung on as long as possible but eventually felt his body go limp as his mind aimlessly pulled up ideas and events and imagery.

Soon he was running from something undefinable, but terrifying. One tormented dream lead to another but finally he was able to make some sense of one. There was a group of people, not normal, but not typical monster fare either, with unknown and beyond-human powers, and they were chasing him. He had a hard time visualizing these entities, they didn't have shape and form like you would normally experience but he could feel them behind him, coming for him. If he turned around he could only see a vague presence, much like looking at something with your peripheral vision.

Bob was alone, in a big office building, running from room to room until he burst through a door into a gigantic factory that covered acres. It was dark and he could barely make his way without running into industrial machines, parts, tools and work stations. He found a cart on a small rail system that was used to transport the things that were manufactured. He jumped on and pushed off, using the single car as if it were a sled racing downhill on a winter's day. It was too dark to see where he was going as it weaved between obstacles. There was a sense of relief as the car reached roller coaster speeds until he could feel himself traveling in a large circle as if the track were arranged in a downward spiral. There was no time to formulate an escape plan before hearing a sharp pop, as if he were standing on the trap door of a hangman's platform, and suddenly he was falling into blinding, white light.

Bob bolted upright drenched in sweat, feeling nauseous and disoriented but sitting in his bed, in his bedroom. The faint early morning light illuminated a familiar neighborhood. He wondered, Did I just cheat death? He didn't know.

It clearly wasn't his time, he thought, not yet. But would it soon be?

She held me tight

I was unavailable and she knew it.

Amy and I met her through a friend. We would see her at social gatherings: friend's parties, fund raisers, gallery openings and the like. She and I had similar jobs so we could talk shop. Eventually Amy would wander away.

She was attractive, eclectic and funny, but I was with someone I loved. Amy was the woman I had bonded to and was comfortable with. I was happy and wasn't going to do anything to ruin that. Still, she was intriguing and it was always good to see her.

Besides work, our conversations included a variety of topics, I thought relationships were just one of them. It was always generalized, never about the person we were with but quite specific: the good, the bad, the pet peeves, the things that would definitely make you walk away.

I had no idea she was taking it all in– books I'd read, things I'd done, favorites I'd mentioned. I never noticed she was watching me with Amy or when an attractive girl would catch my eye. Later, I complimented her on it, but had no idea she had changed the color of her hair, for me.

She was much better at this than I realized. One night I leaned in to give her a friendly hug and she pulled me close and tight. A couple of days later it took a while, but I finally realized it was the faint, sweet smell that was triggering the memories of her. It was very light but I would catch it time and again through out the day. I bent my head forward, grabbed the sweater and pulled it to my nose. That was it. I was wearing the sweater she had rubbed herself up against. The one she knew I would wear again before washing. The one she knew would retain her floral perfume and the memory of her. She was so casual, so clever, I was never aware.

When we'd see her, it seemed like she was with someone different every time. I figured finding someone to accompany her was never a problem. She would frequently say, "He's just a coworker," or something like that when her date would go for drinks. I thought, It's okay to date people you work with. I never made the connection. One guy, Roger, and I hit it off. I saw him at a bar once when I was with friends. He said that they had only gone out a few times before she told him she didn't like him "...that way." He said he thought she was pining away for someone else. We tried to figure it out, I had no idea.

Late one night at a friend's party after many had already left, I saw Amy flirting with someone's date. As I watched her from the corner of my eye, I grew apprehensive as she kept poking at him then put her hand on his shoulder and leaned in too far.

I walked over when he went to refresh his drink and with half a smile said, "Hi."

She spun around in an exaggerated manner barely keeping her balance and with a big smile said, "Hi!"

"What are you doing?"

"I'm being charming and funny with someone else while you try to decide what you want in life."

"What?"

I chalked it up to far more alcohol than usual and at the time had no idea what she was talking about. The next day when I asked her, Amy said she couldn't remember the incident, or much that happened after 11:00 that night.

A couple of weeks later, after the opening of an exhibit for one of our friends, I was surprised when Amy said "We talked about *you!*" in a snide manner as we were getting ready for bed. Their conversation was in the context of casual relationship talk, the way women compare their mates. But Amy knew, I didn't.

She didn't put an end to us, but by that time, the relationship that I thought might last forever had changed in a number of ways and Amy was ready to move on.

You see, I was unavailable and she knew it.
Then I wasn't, and I didn't stand a chance.

Pause

It's raining. I look down a few stories to streets that are glossy, trees without leaves, neatly aligned rows of cars and bobbing umbrellas making their way toward the entrance. I think of the people I passed on my way up as I stare off into the hazy shimmer of falling rain:

> A young woman with a phone to her ear, argues with her
> boyfriend about weekend plans–
> "No, we're going to the play.
> Yes, you have to come.
> Because I went to the hockey game last week."
> Professionals in uniforms reading through paperwork as they
> wait for the elevator.
> The curly hair and round face of the always cheerful woman
> who works at the coffee shop.
> The stoic security guard, most likely counting down the hours
> until he can go home to his wife and son.

Then I turn around and see my mother lying there with an oxygen mask and heart monitor, eyes closed. Muted light comes through the window and falls on her creating light gray shadows. The only sound is the steady beat of the monitor.

I project ahead to a time that if not tomorrow, or this week, is not very far away. A funeral, a house, a car, a lifetime of possessions. Furniture, clothes, jewelry, appliances, photographs... and more photographs and more of distant relatives I never met with names written in cursive on the back that I don't recognize. In the next box on the top of the stack, a spelling test from the first grade.

cat

mop

boy

100% in red pen alongside a rubber-stamped star. I see my name on the top in rough, rigid letters each vertical, horizontal and rounded stroke painstakingly controlled.

When I was in high school I visited the room of my first grade class. The desks were so small I had a hard time imagining I was ever that tiny. I remembered that when my niece entered first grade. Her youngest now sits in one of those desks.

I sift through a lifetime of possessions, a catalog of experiences, a document of her existence, and as I try to decide what to do with it all, realize as time pushes me forward there will be a moment when someone is doing this with my things.

I what say hears I she

After many months, when I think I know her well enough and she knows quite a bit about me, I say something like, "Look at how blue the sky is today," and she says, "Why don't you like tomato soup?"

At first I thought this was a communication issue, but it's not. I'm not speaking a foreign language. We are both relatively bright. I am enunciating, there are no disruptive noises that might make hearing difficult. In fact, she could repeat what I said, verbatim. It's just that often I say something and she hears something else. It certainly feels like it's a serious neurological problem one or both of us are having, but when she talks to her friends about it, they agree with her and when I talk to my friends they agree with me.

When this happens I go into great detail about what I'm trying to express not just logically, but emotionally too, in case she is one of those people who can only understand feelings– which she isn't, unless I don't know her as well as I think I do.

This wouldn't bother me at all, these minor blips if they didn't escalate to anger or melancholy, for her, though sometimes for me as well as she takes me down this path. An innocent statement, misconstrued, is a nuisance, until I find myself trying to rectify the quagmire at the end of this dance. It is not surprising that it usually ends, unresolved, in silence.

Unbearable

When you find yourself engulfed in what could be a potential catastrophe, the moments leading up to it, even those earlier in the day, are routine, nondescript, hardly an omen of impending doom.

I was on a long road trip and had stopped to spend a few days in Teton National Park, just south of Yellowstone. I set up camp at Jenny Lake and planned to hike from the Lupine Meadows Trailhead to Amphitheater Lake the next day. It's a 5 mile trek uphill with a 3000 foot elevation gain. The National Park literature rates this 10 mile round-trip excursion as, STRENUOUS. I guess the use of capital letters is a polite way for the Park Service to say, "All of you tourists who think you are in good shape? You're not."

The air was cool as I started up the trail midmorning. There were young, eager hikers that passed me and a few hikers I passed, most of them sitting on the side of the trail taking a break. I was hiking alone but never seemed to be out of sight of someone either ahead of me or behind.

An hour and a half into the hike I came to the junction where another trail splits off and heads toward Bradley Lake. After that I noticed fewer people, in fact, almost none. It's a long, slow, uphill grind and I had to guess that many took the other trail or just got tired and turned around.

Eventually I was hiking in solitude, pacing myself and enjoying the stately serenity. The sun had been out for most of the day but as I came close to my destination, clouds moved in and the air became cool. Finally I stepped up to the point where I could see the lake. While the official trail ends here it is the jumping off point for climbers who want to scale the Grand Teton or other peaks in the area. I saw a couple of tents that were abandoned, obviously waiting for their owners to come back, victorious or dejected. Even though it was two weeks before the official start of summer and nearly everywhere in the country it was warm to heatstroke, there were still large icebergs floating in the lake and remnants of massive snowdrifts tucked beneath the biggest trees. Low, heavy clouds obscured the view and now a smattering of rain drops fell. As I hiked around the small lake, the rain turned to snow and as nice as it looked falling gently on tree limbs and floating onto the surface of the water, I was ready to head back.

The snow turned to light rain again, then stopped shortly after I left. The trail wound back and forth as it zigzagged through the forest. I was surprised it had been so long since I had seen other hikers and it seemed like I now had the whole trail to myself. I finally came to the junction where the trail splits, and up to that point I was having a hard time charting my progress. Now, I was a little less than two miles from the car.

About 15 minutes later, while my mind was wandering and vaguely aware of little more than the trail ahead of me, I heard an animal crash through the underbrush. It only takes a fraction of a second to determine whether it's a small creature like a chipmunk, or something larger. This was much larger, and I instantly snapped my head to the right. Off in the brush, slightly uphill from me was a bear, sitting like a frog, neck extended, ears perked up, staring at me. Only 30 feet away.

If there had been steel bars or four inch thick, bullet proof glass between us, I might have thought, "Awwww… How cute!" But there wasn't and I was nearly paralyzed. I knew not to run, but couldn't think of any other option. My mind was clouded with fear, mesmerized by our stare-off. I had no idea what would happen next, until…

All of a sudden the bear charged. He jumped on top of me, we wrestled around, I got him in a headlock, gave him a knuckle sandwich, let him go, kicked him in the ass and he ran into the woods never to be seen again.

They call me Tarzan of the Tetons. But that's on the down low, so don't spread it around.

Ok, ok.

What really happened is that I started walking slowly, averting my gaze, and using my peripheral vision to see if the bear had moved. It seemed as if he was as surprised and confused as me, except I hardly think his heart was beating so hard it was about to crack his rib cage, like mine was. I methodically picked up my pace until the trail curved to the right and sloped down. As soon as he was out of sight, I ran. Periodically I would look over my shoulder, but I ran until I was exhausted.

10 minutes later, I abruptly stopped and said out loud, "Oh, my God." I was looking through a clearing at a small lake and realized I was on the wrong trail. At the junction I had taken the wrong fork, and worse, had to go back past the point where I had encountered the bear to get to the main trail that lead to the parking lot. I was dumbfounded.

I thought of going off trail, and just cutting through the forest. I knew what direction I had to go in, but the combination of underbrush, trees, and uneven terrain seemed daunting. If I came to a cliff and had to hike sideways instead of forward, the opportunity to get lost was great. It just didn't seem like a good idea.

I started to walk back along the trail with various scenarios running through my head: "Hey, it's just me again. No need to stop eating berries, or anything. Just passing through." Then I wondered if it would be possible to engage a bear with the idea of simply avoiding consumption. I thought about what it takes to grab a mouse. Although superior size, strength, and intelligence are on my side, if I'm chasing a mouse through my kitchen, there is a good chance he is going to get away. Is there some kind of, Lessons Of The Mouse, that I could apply in a zen-like fashion to avoid certain death? Hmmm… Was there a more feasible and slightly less esoteric idea that I could come up with instead?

As I walked back, I thought about the encounter. The bear didn't exhibit any kind of threatening behavior nor was he curious enough to come closer. Park Rangers often advise hikers to make noise as they walk, in order to alert wildlife that you are coming. Wild animals might attack if they are suddenly spooked but are rarely the savage, aggressive beasts that the media make them out to be.

So I started singing. Funny thing, I couldn't remember all the words to any song and for most, there was a lot of, la, la, la, after the first few words until I could hit the chorus. I sounded like a really bad mix tape of cover bands doing popular tunes. If this is an effective technique to alert and drive away wildlife, I think I would have scared away humans as well.

I finally came to the part of the trail that I recognized. It curved up and to the left and I slowed while continuing my vocal display of song, but by this point, I was throwing in bits of poetry and memorable speeches, too. My eyes scanned the forest and it appeared the coast was clear. I proceeded, but looked like a bird, my head nervously jerking and spinning around, eyeing every nuance and anomaly. The forest was calm, the sun was back out and everything seemed fine.

Until...

I passed a certain tree, and the bear, from high above, pounced on my back, we wrestled around, I got him in a headlock, gave him a knuckle sandwich, let him go, kicked him in the ass and it was *then*, that he ran into the woods never to be seen again.

I swear to God, Tarzan of the Tetons.

Ok, ok.

Fine.

The coast was clear, I made it back to the junction and got on the segment of the trail heading toward the car. I arrived safe and sound an hour or so later.

Happy? Good.

I still like my version better.

Undone

It's been long enough, perhaps too long. The little things that helped create and strengthen the bond, the deep attachment to her, have to be undone. I've let them linger, thinking there might be a change, thinking it may be easier this way, thinking there was some comfort in it.

No.

I take out my phone. The cover photo is that great picture of her staring right at me with a smile on her face. I delete it and will now be greeted by stormy clouds over a grassy plain. In my contacts, I take her off of the favorites list.

I do the same with the tablet, then pull the screen saver on the computer, the one with the photos of us at parties, on holidays, on vacation, taken with friends and family. Pictures around the house are lifted off the end table, the night stand, the bureau. Her photo comes out of my wallet.

This shirt and that one too, those shoes, suit, tie… maybe I can spare my favorite pants– no, those too, it looks like a good quarter of my clothes are gifts from her. I pull open the drawers one by one and sift through the contents. There's an old sweatshirt of hers and a sweater she never wore, and one of her fancy bras. Did she leave that on purpose, to taunt me? No, it certainly is not one of my favorites, I was never a fan of kelly green. She left it because she couldn't get away from me fast enough– ha, ha. My clothes go in a box, I can't quite bring myself to give them to charity. Hers are stacked on the bed. The box goes in the basement. In the storage room. The back of the storage room.

The cup she always used- would anyone want that? It was easy enough to toss it into the wastebasket. That seems to break the ice. Those two cookbooks with a few recipes we marked, that she wanted to make together but we never got around to, hit the bottom of the can with a thud. That dumb spatula, swish. Same for that stupid can opener she bought. Where was the good one? The one I had bought years ago? Did she throw it out? I can open a can with a screw driver and a pair of tin snips, I'm not using that idiotic device anymore.

Her favorite paring knife that she got in Berlin (why didn't she take that?), hits the rim and bounces on the floor. I stare at it and think, Maybe she would want that. Maybe this is a sign, divine intervention, that would give her pause to reconsider as I gallantly show up and present her with it, and the other things she left. She would see what a great guy I am, how kind and considerate.

What in the hell am I thinking?

No, don't break the rhythm. The save-the-date card for her cousin's wedding that is attached to the side of the refrigerator and the butterfly magnet that holds it in place, the monthly calendar– nope, there's nothing on there that I wrote, grab them all and toss.

Her toothbrush plops into the bathroom trash. All of the things she bought, that are in the medicine cabinet, I've used too. The hand lotion, the body lotion (because, heaven forbid, you can't use hand lotion on your body or vice versa! I shake my head back and forth at the apparent foolishness of her logic), the lip balm, the floss, the aspirin alternative that I only started to use because she bought and recommended it, the special whitening toothpaste. It would be foolish to get rid of these things, yet when I stare at them I see her in an oversized tee shirt, the kind she uses as a nightgown, brushing her teeth. I see her crawling across the bed while I'm lying on my back, moving closer until I can taste her minty breath.

In a series of rapid fire motions they all end up in the bottom of the waste can. The plastic liner is pulled, I grab the clothes on the bed and the liner from the kitchen and walk them to the large trash barrel in the garage.

The bedroom that I painted for her, because she liked that color and it felt good to both surprise and please her, has to be changed.

Standing motionless, staring at hundreds of swatches I'm not really looking for a color as much as a solution to dull the pain. Nothing looks good, nothing is interesting. Twilight Sensation is as bland as Sunrise Spectacle. It was white before, might as well be white again.

Three coats to fully cover it. It would have gone faster if I hadn't plopped down on the edge of the bed so often, each time letting out a big sigh, then finding it hard to stand up and keep painting.

When everything is back to the way it was before, the way I used to like it, the way that brought contentment and comfort when I came home, now it just feels empty.

It's the little things

I hate it when the toast pops up and it's overdone. It comes out of the toaster like a piece of styrofoam. When I try to butter it, it breaks into pieces, when I eat it, it disintegrates into crumbs. I only remember to turn down the setting on the toaster at this moment but I'm hungry and mad I didn't do it before, and since this is a regular irritant, something that has been going on for a while, I know that'll I remember to do it this time. I'm sure of it. Just as soon as I'm done.

But when I'm done with coffee and reading and toast my mind is on to the next thing and when I first wake up I'm not coherent beyond my breakfast-making routine to have the mental capacity to think of anything else. So this goes on day after day but only until the loaf is gone and then I buy a more hearty one, the kind that can stand up to the heat. At this point the problem would be solved except I balk at the price and eventually buy the cheaper stuff and it starts all over.

It sounds like madness, something so easy to control when so much in our lives is out of our control, but when it happens, this one little thing, over weeks or months and is not condensed into a couple of paragraphs, the experience of living it is much different than the experience of reading about it.

I'm an expert

I was set up with an attractive woman and we hit it off right away. The only thing I was told about her was that we shared some hobbies so I started talking about that. It was going well and eventually I asked what she did for a living.

"I'm a sex expert." She said it like she was telling me she sold insurance. She did it without flinching or looking away or hesitating. This was unexpected and I was having a hard time responding because I was trying to process two different things at one time. First, if things continued to go well, the idea of having sex with someone I liked, found attractive, and was probably pretty good in bed. Second, how do you make money doing that? It was way too early to say, "That sounds fantastic and I can't wait to have sex with you," so I went with the second one.

"I'm on the radio and I write an advice column that a few newspapers run." She told me the call sign of the local station she was on, but I didn't recognize it.

"It's a small, talk-only, station."

She seemed at ease with talking about this so I was compelled to ask her more.

"What does it take to be a sex expert? I mean, do you need a medical degree?"

"That's one way to approach it, but just because you understand anatomy doesn't mean you understand sex. Sex is more complicated than that."

"But you've studied human anatomy, or biology, or things like that?"

"Sure, a little."

"Psychology?"

"A bit."

"But you have some kind of college degree in something that is specifically related to this subject?"

"No," she said in a nonchalant manner. "What matters is your knowledge of the subject."

"But without some kind of specific program or degree how do you measure how much you've learned in order to qualify as an expert?"

"My readers and callers ask questions and I provide them with answers. Someone who wasn't an expert couldn't do that."

"Well, saying you are an expert certainly makes you sound more knowledgeable than just having a degree," I said with a tinge of sarcasm.

"It is. My knowledge is more well rounded. It comes from workshops and seminars– so lectures, but hands on stuff, too. And I learn things from reading and studying other experts and just talking to people."

"So, they have hands-on seminars teaching these things?"

"Yes, there are all sorts of seminars and I pick the ones that I think will apply to what I'm doing and need to know."

"Like what?

"There was this great workshop I attended recently where I had my pussy massaged for 45 minutes. It was fantastic."

I smiled.

"What?"

"It's funny, because this sounds like one of those sleazy things a man would say, 'Honey, this great looking blond had to give me a hand job. I'm a sex expert and it's my job.'"

"It's not like that. People look to me for advice and answers to questions about sex. I get all kinds of questions and I have to know about this stuff."

It was odd to think that she was justifying sexual encounters with strangers as a mandatory requirement of her job, if the stranger happened to be an instructor. Yet there are plenty of men who pay for sex, and many who have casual sex with people they barely know, so who am I to judge. It wasn't so much the sex issue that was bothersome as much as it was the assertion of expertise.

It seems like there are experts popping up everywhere for all kinds of things and many are people who have a questionable background in the area in which they are claiming expertise. Yet once they call themselves an expert everyone treats them as if they know infinitely more about a subject than everyone else. And worse, our culture feels the need to seek out the advice of these so-called experts, deferring to the expert's judgment over their own or those around them.

"But how do you qualify yourself as a sex *expert*? Simply your ability to answer questions about sex?" I still couldn't understand what separated her from just anyone giving out advice.

"Through my knowledge and experience."

"What I'm saying is that your portrayal as an expert doesn't have the things that one would normally expect to back it up. There is no nationally sanctioned program that you had to complete to get officially recognized certification. There is no two or four year accredited course of study in which you get a degree. You just call yourself an expert and then people think you have special qualifications."

"It's not like that."

"But it's easy enough for someone to make up something, then declare that they are an expert in it. For example, I could start to refer to myself as…" I tried to think of something that could be seen as both legitimate and silly, "a dessert expert. And make other people recognize me as such. I like sweet food and I've eaten plenty of desserts. I just have to familiarize myself with the desserts I'm unaware of, and I'm an expert."

"You can't just declare yourself an expert without any knowledge of that subject."

"Actually I can. In fact, this will be my coming out moment, my official proclamation. I am a dessert expert!"

"No you're not."

"Yes I am," I said with a pompous tone and a flair for the dramatic. "I declared I was, and thus I am."

"And when someone asks for your qualifications and education, what are you going to tell them?"

"That I attended the... Culinary School of Exotic Desserts, and Fine Cooking, and Culinary Expertise!"

"Is that even a real place?"

"It must be! It has the word, expertise, in it's name!"

"That's not funny." She looked away with disgust, and folded her arms across her chest. A moment later she turned back toward me and said, "The pussy massage was important because it adds to my overall knowledge and allows me to answer questions that my listeners and readers ask. I really have to do these things because as a sex expert, it's my job to know about things like this."

"Really? You really have people call you up and ask, 'I've never had someone massage my pussy for 45 minutes, is that any fun?'"

"Well…" She looked at me as if she were trying to find some useful way she could justify the pussy massage, not just this particular thing, but any other opportunity like this that might come up in the future.

"This is like me saying that as a dessert expert I have to go out and eat four gallons of ice cream, not because I want to, but because it's my job!"

"It's not the same thing," she insisted.

"Sure it is. Because I never know when one of my callers—"

"You think it's easy to get a radio show?" You think you could get your own show?"

"Yes, and syndicated column too, because," and then with a slightly sarcastic tone, "I'm an expert. And I never know when someone might call me up and say, (I went into a mock conversation as if I was on the air) 'I've never tried ice cream is it any good?'

First, I'd have to give the universal expert disclaimer: 'Well, it's possible some people might not like it, and you should always check with your doctor first,' then I could get to the nitty-gritty, 'but most people who've tried it LOVE IT! They can't get enough of it, want to eat it night and day.'

'Really?'

'And it comes in different flavors, I don't know if you are aware of that.'

'I had no idea!'

'Yes. So if you like coconut or blueberries or chocolate chips there are ice creams with those things in them. I hope that helps you out.'

'Wow, you're amazing! I'm so glad I called.'

'And thank you for asking an expert because if you had asked just anyone you certainly wouldn't have been able to trust their opinion.'"

She was looking at me with a scowl on her face.

I kept going. "And because I'm a dessert expert I have to regularly eat ice cream, so I can stay on the forefront of ice cream news. I may go into a euphoric, sugar-induced coma, but it's a small price to pay for my profession."

"There is no such thing as a dessert expert," she said dismissively. "The very idea is ridiculous."

I looked at her with arched eyebrows, my head slightly tilted, arms extended to the side with my palms upward.

"I *am* a sex expert!" She screamed. "It's a legitimate occupation!"

"I'm sorry I can't have this conversation now, I have to run out and get some ice cream. I mean, you never know when all the ice cream making companies all over the world are just gonna stop making good ice cream, but if that day ever comes then I have to be on top of it so I can inform all my readers and listeners. But first," I turn away from her slightly and place my hand lightly over my ear, "Next caller please."

I imitate a southern drawl, "Hello. I've never had cheese cake, is it any good?"

"Well, as an expert…"